THE AMISH CAFE

Amish Romance

HANNAH MILLER

D1715231

Tica House
Publishing

Sweet Romance that Delights and Enchants!

Copyright © 2023 by Tica House Publishing LLC

All rights reserved.

No part of this book may be reproduced in any form or by any electronic or mechanical means, including information storage and retrieval systems, without written permission from the author, except for the use of brief quotations in a book review.

Personal Word from the Author

To My Dear Readers,

How exciting that you have chosen one of my books to read. Thank you! I am proud to now be part of the team of writers at Tica House Publishing who work joyfully to bring you stories of hope, faith, courage, and love.

Please feel free to contact me as I love to hear from my readers. I would like to personally invite you to sign up for updates and to become part of our **Exclusive Reader Club** —it's completely Free to join! Hope to see you there!

With love,

Hannah Miller

VISIT HERE to Join our Reader's Club and to Receive Tica House Updates:

https://amish.subscribemenow.com/

Contents

Chapter One

Dorothy sat quietly in the fields as the dry wind danced past, causing the grass at her feet to tickle her skin. The birds chirped around her, and the warm setting sun cast a golden glow on her peaceful surroundings. She fixed her gaze on the horizon with endless rows of crops swaying ever-so-slightly in the playful breeze and wondered if anything about her life would ever change.

Dorothy knew what she had to do and what her community expected: find a husband, settle down, and start having children. The only problem was that whenever she saw all her friends doing this, her stomach turned uncomfortably, and her palms began sweating.

"Dorothy... Dorothy!"

Dorothy's head shot up at the sound of her name, pulling her out of her sad, anxious thoughts. She turned to see her mother standing outside the barn door, squinting against the setting sun, looking for her.

Dorothy murmured, "Coming, *Mamm*," as she rose to her feet, wiping her sweaty palms while brushing the dirt from her skirts. She approached the house and her waiting mother.

"There you are," Bernice said as she saw her daughter walking toward her.

Dorothy gave her mother a fond smile. "I'm here. What do you need?"

Bernice studied Dorothy curiously for a moment before she nodded. "It's about time we started on dinner." She turned and walked back into the house.

Dorothy frowned briefly at her mother's strange behavior before she shrugged and followed Bernice into the kitchen.

"So, what's the plan for dinner?" Dorothy inquired as she scrubbed her hands at the kitchen sink. The water from the cold tap was lukewarm after spending a long, warm day in the pipes.

"Nothing fancy, just some casserole. I don't have much energy for anything more than that."

"That's fine, *Mamm*; it shouldn't take long." Dorothy wiped her hands on a nearby dishtowel and walked over to the kitchen counter. She then took a knife from the drawer and an onion from the vegetable rack before rolling up her sleeves and getting to work. "I can even make it myself if you'd like to rest."

Bernice shook her head as she began gathering the remaining ingredients. "No need, *liebchen*, I enjoy cooking."

They worked in companionable silence for a few moments. But the more Dorothy observed her mother out of the corner of her eye, the more she realized something was obviously wrong. Bernice walked slowly and carefully as if each step caused her pain, and her brows were furrowed firmly over her tired eyes. And the more Dorothy thought about it, the more she realized how long it had been since she'd seen her mother with a smile instead of a deep frown. Try as she might, Dorothy could not recall when she last saw her mother smile.

Bernice had also been mentioning lately how she had no energy to do things. Dorothy had chalked it up to her mother being tired after a long day of work. Bernice helped their Amish community however she could, whether by cooking, cleaning, or looking after the children of various members. Work had been picking up significantly due to the recent start of the summer holidays, which was helpful for income but seemed to be taking a toll on Bernice's health.

Dorothy had also always assumed her mother's constant discomfort stemmed from her father's tragic death many years earlier, but now she wasn't so sure.

Dorothy was at a loss as to what to do. Should she check in constantly with her mother to see if she was all right? Or should she keep an eye on things while leaving her mother alone? Dorothy didn't want to upset her mother by asking if there was anything wrong, but she needed to know if there was a problem.

She wished her best friend, Moriah, lived next door or was easier to reach at times like these. However, as much as she wanted to, Dorothy couldn't drop everything she was doing and take the ten-minute buggy ride to visit her best friend to share her concerns about her mother.

Dorothy sighed and sniffled before wiping her eyes with the back of her hand as she realized the onions were quite strong. As she wiped another tear from her cheek, she resolved to concentrate fully on the task at hand. Otherwise, she could end up cutting her finger or something equally painful. Now was not the time to see things that weren't there.

Her mother was in good health.

She had to be.

Dorothy shook her head and resisted the urge to sigh as the tightness in her chest increased at the mere thought of the nightmare that would be the alternative.

Bernice started softly humming as she assembled the ingredients for dinner as if to prove her daughter's worry was for nothing, and Dorothy's shoulders began to relax.

There was nothing to be concerned about.

Mother and daughter continued to work silently for a short while as Dorothy chopped the vegetables and added various flavorings, and Bernice mixed the casserole ingredients. In less than twenty minutes, the casserole was in the oven.

Later, they sat at the smooth, rustic dining table that Dorothy's great-great-great grandfather had created with his own hands out of the log from a giant tree. Dorothy and Bernice each had a plate of delicious, hearty food and a glass of water in front of them as they said the silent blessing.

"So, *Mamm*, how was your day?" Dorothy asked after prayer. Her stomach rumbled impatiently. She hadn't realized how hungry she was until they had started making dinner. Her mouth watered as the fragrant steam from her plate wafted playfully beneath her nose. She barely had the patience to blow on the food before eating it.

"It was *gut,* thank you, *liebchen*," Bernice replied as she idly moved her food around the plate with her spoon. She seemed utterly disinterested in eating anything. In fact, she looked somewhat like she was feeling ill.

"I'm glad to hear that." For a few moments, the only sound in the room was the clinking of Dorothy's spoon on the edge of her plate as she took mouthfuls of food.

"And how was your day?" Bernice eventually asked as she shook her head like she was pulling herself out of her thoughts. She seemed wholly distracted.

"It was *gut* for me, too. I managed to sell a couple more things at the tourist shop, and I've gotten started on more projects that clients requested." Ever since Dorothy could hold a needle, she'd been selling handmade items to the local tourist shop. She didn't earn much from it, but it kept her busy, and she was grateful for what little she did earn.

"Oh, that's wonderful *gut* news." Bernice managed to smile before pushing her plate away. "I'm full," she murmured, but Dorothy had been watching closely and knew her mother hadn't taken more than a few bites.

Dorothy took a deep breath. This wasn't the first night that Bernice hadn't eaten much of anything, so she decided had no choice but to ask the question on her mind. "Are you truly okay, *Mamm*?"

"Hmm?" Bernice replied distractedly. "Oh, *jah*, I'm fine. Just more tired than hungry, that's all."

Dorothy shook her head. "*Nee, Mamm*, that's not it. I've seen you. You look like you're in pain, and you're barely eating. Is there something wrong?"

For a moment, Bernice looked like she might say something important, but then she shook her head. "*Nee*, there's nothing wrong. It's just that since your father died, things have been so difficult..."

Dorothy's father had died over two decades ago in an accident during a barn raising, and Dorothy knew that couldn't possibly be the whole issue. While Bernice had always been sad, she hadn't had any problems coping with daily life until lately.

"I know that," Dorothy replied, deciding not to push the issue. She reached over to squeeze her mother's calloused fingers. "I know you miss him. Even though I barely knew him, I miss him, too. But goodness, it was a long time ago."

Bernice sighed heavily. "I wish you could somehow find the same happiness I had with him."

Dorothy pulled her hand back. *"Nee, Mamm,* I'd rather live as a spinster with a bunch of cats above a café that I own and run myself. I've no interest in marrying."

Bernice frowned, looking stunned. "A café? I don't know where you got this café idea. You should stay here with the community that knows and loves you rather than venturing into unfamiliar territory with the *Englischers.* You know the *Englisch* can be ... dangerous."

Dorothy sighed; this was not the first time they'd had this conversation, nor would it be the last time. She'd missed out on her *Rumspringa,* choosing instead to stay and help her widowed mother, but from the stories people had told,

Dorothy knew to stay away from the *Englischers*. Her heart fluttered, and her feet tapped impatiently; her restlessness surged unexpectedly within her. "I know, *Mamm*, but there's so much more for me out there."

"*Nee*, Dorothy, listen to me." After raising her voice slightly, Bernice winced in pain but then tried to neutralize her expression just as quickly. "You must stay here, find a nice man, settle down, and have a big family, just like I wanted, but never could. Promise me you'll do that. Promise me that when I'm gone, you'll do that."

Dorothy's eyebrows shot up into her hairline. "When *you're gone*? What are you talking about? You're still young. You're not going anywhere. You *can't* go anywhere. What will I do if you go before I'm ready?"

"Life is fleeting, *liebchen*," Bernice replied as she lifted her hand and brushed her fingers over her daughter's cheek. "And you'll never be ready for me to go. But when it's my time to rejoin the Lord, it's my time. There is nothing we can do to prevent His wishes."

"You're scaring me, *Mamm*," Dorothy said, her voice breaking as tears closed her throat and welled in her eyes. "How will I cope if you—"

"I'm sorry, Dorothy," Bernice interrupted tiredly with a shake of her head as she picked up her plate full of food and got to her feet. "But it's life."

Dorothy nodded. "I-I know... *Dat* was the perfect example of how fleeting and unexpected life can be. But you're okay?"

Bernice didn't reply. Instead, she walked toward the kitchen, one slow, laborious step at a time.

"*Mamm?*" Dorothy queried as she grabbed her empty dish and followed her mother.

"Of course, *liebchen*. I'm just fine."

As she studied her mother's tired eyes, and her barely-there smile, Dorothy couldn't help but wonder if her mother was lying to her.

Thankfully, Dorothy didn't have to wait too long before seeing her best friend again, as Moriah decided to visit her the next day.

"Hello, Moriah," Dorothy called with a wave as she stood by the front door of their barn. She'd heard the steady clip-clop of the horse's hooves coming up the driveway. Dorothy had shot to her feet and rushed to the door before blocking the sun from her eyes as she excitedly watched her friend arrive. "What brings you by today?" Dorothy tried to sound nonchalant about seeing Moriah, but inside, she was overjoyed.

Moriah shrugged as she kissed her father, who had driven her, and stepped down from the buggy.

"I feel like I haven't seen you in ages, and I know how much you like surprises."

Dorothy ducked her head with a smile on her face. "You know me too well."

Moriah nodded and linked her arm with her friend's as they reached the house. "So, how have things been going?" she asked as they walked into the kitchen together.

"*Mamm* is currently caring for Mr. Kaufman's *kinner*, and I was just finishing a project..." Dorothy's tone turned apologetic as she took in the mess of felt, wool, thread, glue, a small wooden figure, and various other crafting supplies scattered over the kitchen table. "If I'd known you were coming, I would have cleaned up a bit."

"It's okay, Dorothy. I should have warned you ahead of time."

Dorothy shrugged, and there were a few moments of companionable silence between the two friends before Dorothy remembered her manners. "Can I get you anything?"

"A glass of water would be perfect, thank you. The road was dusty, and my throat is parched."

Dorothy nodded, and within a few moments the two friends sat at the table, a glass of water before each of them.

"It's so nice that you've come to visit," Dorothy said as she took a sip from her glass.

Moriah shrugged as she took a sip of water herself. "I just had the strangest feeling I needed to talk with you."

"Well, you're not wrong," Dorothy said before sighing as she decided how exactly to tell her friend what was on her mind.

"Is everything all right?" Moriah questioned gently after her friend had gone silent for a while.

"Mm?" Dorothy murmured distractedly. "Remember how I always say that I want to live in a little place above a café that I own and run myself?"

"*Jah*, of course, I remember," Moriah replied with a firm nod.

" *Mamm* doesn't want me to do that. She wants me to stay here, find a nice man to settle down with, and start a family. And I know I'm supposed to do that, but I don't... I can't..." Dorothy cleared her throat and stared into space as she felt tears of frustration prickle behind her eyes.

Moriah was quiet for a moment before reaching forward and gently squeezing Dorothy's wrist. "Follow your heart," she eventually said simply.

Dorothy nodded and exhaled loudly, resisting the urge to sniff. She had known Moriah would be on her side.

"And I would be happy to join you," Moriah continued with a shudder. "I have absolutely no interest in following our district's expectations either."

"Eli is still ignoring you, then?" Dorothy queried as she played with a droplet of water that had slipped down the side of her glass to settle on the wooden surface of the table.

Moriah ducked her head and blinked rapidly, a sign that Dorothy recognized quickly as distress in her friend. "Well, he doesn't know what he's missing out on."

Moriah laughed and sniffled before pulling a handkerchief out of her sleeve and wiping her slightly reddened nose. "Thank you, Dorothy. I knew you were my friend for a reason."

Dorothy nodded before sighing again. She desperately wanted to tell someone about her worries regarding her mother, but she wasn't sure if it was her place to discuss them with anyone outside the family.

"Why are you sighing so much, anyway? It's like you have the weight of the world on your shoulders," Moriah queried, and those few words were enough to encourage the floodgates to open.

"I think there's something wrong with *Mamm*."

Moriah's hand flew to her mouth as she audibly gasped. *"Nee,* don't say that. Surely you're mistaken."

"I wish I were." Once again, Dorothy sighed, this time hard enough to blow a stray hair that had slipped out of her *kapp* and hung over her eyes. "Maybe I'm just seeing things. I don't know."

"Why don't you tell me what you've seen, and I'll try to help."

Dorothy took a deep breath before launching into her concerns. "It started with just the little things, like forgetting where she put her glasses, being unable to read something, or misplacing her knitting. But now there are the mood swings— she can be completely normal one moment, and the next, she's snapping at me for no reason. And she is so tired and moves so slowly like she's in pain. Not to mention, sometimes, she seems so distant, like she's not really here."

Dorothy sighed as she pinched the bridge of her nose, trying to control the emotions she could feel rising inside her. "I thought it was all because of grief. She has hung onto that for years and years, my whole life, truly. She's not been the same since *Dat* died, and I can't remember much what she was like before that, but I know it's gotten worse in the past three months."

Moriah's expression was sympathetic as she listened to Dorothy's worries. "It could be nothing, just normal aging. Your *mamm* is a busy woman, remember? She's juggling three different jobs to provide for the two of you." The young woman bit her lip as she stared thoughtfully into space. "But if you're worried, have you considered talking to someone about it? An *Englisch* doctor or the village healer, maybe?"

Dorothy shook her head. "I've been told many things about the *Englisch,* warned more like. I don't want to make a too big a deal out of my fretting, and I don't want to upset her. But it's been weighing on my mind a lot lately."

Moriah reached over and patted her friend's hand. "It's a difficult situation, but you shouldn't have to carry it alone. I'm here, and we can figure out a way to approach this together."

Dorothy felt some of the weight lift off her shoulders, knowing she had someone to confide in. She smiled gratefully at Moriah, relieved she didn't have to deal with her worries alone. "Thank you. I really appreciate it."

Moriah returned the smile. "Of course. We're friends, and we support each other. I wish I could advise you about talking to your *mamm* about your concerns."

Dorothy shrugged and watched another droplet of condensation run down the side of her glass to pool at the base of it. "I can try, but what if she just keeps denying something is wrong? What if she won't tell me until it's too late?"

"She might not tell you anything," Moriah said. "But first, you need to take a deep breath. Then we can talk about it."

Dorothy nodded before taking some deep, slow breaths. She felt a lot better afterward. Her chest no longer felt like it was too tight to take in air.

"Feel a bit better?" Moriah queried gently.

Dorothy nodded.

"*Gut.* Now, what were you saying about something being too late?"

Chapter Two

Dorothy felt a whole lot better after talking to Moriah about her mother. Her best friend advised her to keep an eye on Bernice but not press the issue or demand any information. It was good advice, but it caused Dorothy to notice more subtle issues regarding her mother.

One evening a few days after Moriah's visit, Dorothy was in the garden, picking some vegetables for their dinner, when her mother appeared at her side. Bernice looked at her with an intensity that made Dorothy feel uneasy, which she was doing more often of late—as if trying to scrutinize her daughter's soul.

"What is it, *Mamm*?" Dorothy asked.

"I was thinking," Bernice began, and by her tone, Dorothy knew exactly what was coming. She took a deep breath to steel herself before her mother said the following words, "I really think you should give courting a proper try."

Dorothy sighed. "*Mamm*, you know how I feel about courting. I'm not ready to think about it right now. I see how much pain you've had without *Dat*. Plus, who would be around to help you if I got married?"

"You could live here with me. I really appreciate all of your help, but I worry about you. I don't want you to end up alone. You know I won't be around forever, as much as I would like to be."

Dorothy sighed and dug her small trowel into the ground before getting to her feet and dusting off her skirt. "As I pointed out the other night, you're only forty-two. You have plenty of years left. And I won't be alone just because I'm not courting or don't have a *beau*. I have Moriah, and I have you."

Bernice frowned. "But what about when I'm gone? You'll need someone to take care of you."

Dorothy's heart sank. She'd had this conversation with her mother, not three nights previously. If Bernice didn't remember, it was not a good sign about the older woman's mental health. "*Mamm*, I'm asking again if you are okay? We had a conversation just like this one a few nights ago. Don't you remember?"

Bernice forced a smile. "Of course, I'm all right. And I remember our conversation. I have a mind like an elephant, remember?"

Dorothy nodded for they had joked about this before, then she bit her lip worriedly as she watched her mother return to the house. Something was not right.

Over the next few days, Bernice seemed more fatigued than usual, and she needed to stop and remember things she had said just a few minutes earlier or sometimes she would trail off mid-sentence.

One afternoon, a few days after their conversation in the garden, Dorothy found her mother in the kitchen, struggling to read a recipe from her cookbook. Bernice's face was scrunched up in concentration, her glasses balanced precariously on the tip of her nose, and she squinted hard at the words.

"Are you struggling to see?" Dorothy asked.

"It appears so," Bernice replied as she cleaned her glasses on her skirt and put them back on before squinting again.

"Do your eyes hurt? Is your vision worsening?" Dorothy asked softly as she touched her mother's shoulder.

"I don't know," Bernice replied, shaking her head. "I've been having trouble reading lately. Maybe I need new glasses." She took her glasses off and looked at them before shrugging. "I just haven't had the time or the money to get my eyes checked lately."

"*Mamm,* you know the district–"

"The district will help pay, *jah,*" Bernice interrupted gently with a nod, "but we already owe the district so much. They have helped us time and time again with the emergency fund. I can't ask for more. I won't."

Dorothy sighed sadly as she wished and prayed with all her aching heart that money wasn't an issue for them. It wasn't the first time she'd had that thought, and it certainly wouldn't be the last time. She'd lived her entire life watching her mother count her pennies before making any financial decisions. And she couldn't remember how many time the district had chipped in and helped for whatever necessities they needed that they couldn't cover themselves.

As she continued to reflect on their circumstances and wished and prayed for a better life for both of them, Dorothy could not stop her concern regarding her mother with each passing day. A few days later, she found Bernice sitting at the kitchen table, staring off into space. She was breathing heavily, her fingers were clenched into fists so tightly in her lap that the skin was going white, and her face was as pale as chalk.

"*Mamm,* what's wrong?" Dorothy asked as she rushed over to her mother, her voice thick and shaking with worry.

Bernice blinked and shook her head, clearly coming back to herself. "Nothing, *liebchen.* I'm just tired. That's all."

Dorothy felt a pang of fear in her chest. She couldn't deny it a moment longer. Her mother was sick, and Bernice was hiding it from her. Dorothy knew she needed to confront her mother, but she didn't know how to force her to confess whatever it was.

Later that day, Dorothy took a deep breath and knocked on her mother's bedroom door. When she didn't get a reply, panic shot through her, and she entered her mother's room. Bernice was sitting on the edge of her bed, her hands folded in her lap. Her lips were moving, but no sound was forthcoming, and Dorothy sighed with relief before standing in the doorway and waiting until her mother finished her prayers.

"I'm sorry to disturb you," Dorothy apologized once the older woman opened her eyes and looked up, "but we need to talk. *Mamm*, I know something's wrong." Dorothy sat on the mattress beside her mother. "I can see it. You're sick, aren't you?"

Bernice ducked her head, her shaking fingers clasped together in her lap. She was clearly wrestling with something, but in the end, she shook her head, and Dorothy's shoulders slumped with disappointment.

"I'm not sick." Bernice jutted her chin out stubbornly and gestured vaguely toward the door. "And unless you have something more important to talk about, I would appreciate it if you could leave me to my prayers."

Dorothy knew a dismissal when she heard one. She ducked her head to hide the tears stinging her eyes and left the room. The last thing she saw was Bernice with her head down, her fingers clenched in a ball in her lap, praying like her life depended on it.

For all Dorothy knew, that could be precisely what she was doing.

It had been a week and a half since Moriah had visited, and Bernice was getting worse with each passing day.

Dorothy's heart ached as she watched her mother slowly deteriorate and struggle to function, even more so than before, but there was nothing she could do about it if Bernice wasn't willing to meet her halfway.

"*Mamm*, I'm back. I found some of those special onions and oranges you love so that we can make a fantastic meal..." Dorothy announced as she returned from the grocer and maneuvered her way into the house with armfuls of heavy supplies. "I've noticed how you haven't been eating so much lately—*Mamm?*"

Dorothy gasped and nearly dropped the groceries taking in the sight before her. Her mother, paler than Dorothy had ever seen her, was sprawled out on the couch with a cloth pressed to her forehead. Her lips were constantly moving, but Bernice wasn't saying anything audible. The fingers pressing the fabric to her head shook uncontrollably, and Dorothy could see tears streaking down her mother's cheeks from under her closed eyelids.

Dorothy put the groceries down quickly before rushing to her mother and crouching at her side. "*Mamm*, what's wrong?"

Dorothy couldn't understand how her mother could look this sick. Earlier, she'd looked pale and uncomfortable, like usual. But there had been a complete change while Dorothy was away.

"I have a terrible headache." Bernice's voice was so soft, Dorothy had to lean close to her lips to hear her.

"How long have you felt this way?" Dorothy demanded.

"Since last night."

Dorothy frowned as she recalled her mother taking slow, painful steps and seeming to be overly sensitive to the light from the lantern the night before, but again, it had become the norm for Bernice. "This isn't good, *Mamm*. I'm going to get Nancy."

Nancy was the village's healer, and she could often make anyone feel better, no matter the symptoms or the illness.

"*Nee*, don't do that. I'm sure I'll be fine," Bernice whispered as she tried to reason with her daughter. Seeing her mother so weak was heartbreaking. Bernice could barely string words together into a coherent sentence.

Dorothy bit her lip and frowned before making her decision. "*Nee*. I'm not listening to you anymore. I'm going to get Nancy."

Bernice shook her head, which wasn't much more than her head twitching from side to side, before trying to sit up. "Don't bother Nancy. I'm sure I'll be fine." The older woman reached out to try and prevent her daughter from leaving, but her grip was so weak that Dorothy quickly and easily extricated herself. She settled the older, sickly woman into the pillows and pulled a blanket over her. It was a reasonably warm night, but Bernice appeared to be shivering in her distress.

"I'm going, *Mamm*. And that's that." Dorothy had never heard herself sounding so authoritative, but she knew, without a doubt, that her mother needed some serious help immediately.

"Can you at least make my towel cold again before you go?" Bernice requested weakly, now giving up all pretense of preventing Dorothy from getting the district's medicinal woman.

"Of course, *Mamm*." Dorothy gently took the cloth from her mother and rushed to the kitchen. Within moments she was back, and the compress was as cold as it could be with water from the pipes the sun had warmed during the day's heat.

As she pressed the cloth to her mother's forehead, Dorothy vowed silently to do everything she could to help Bernice feel better. The fear of losing her mother was overwhelming and all-consuming, and Dorothy had to do something to ensure her mother was okay. She thought about all of the times Bernice had been there for her, listening to her worries and offering words of comfort, and knew that it was now her turn to return the favor. With renewed determination, Dorothy rushed outside, ready to fetch the local healer.

As hard as she tried, Dorothy could not remember how she got to Nancy's house. All she knew was she didn't even stop to get on her bicycle. She certainly didn't take the time to hitch up the buggy. As soon as she was out the front door, she ran as fast as she could, ignoring the growing stitch in her side and the sun sinking lower and lower in the sky.

By the time she'd reached the Beachey house, it had gotten dark, and as she staggered up the driveway, her hand pressed tightly to her side, Dorothy prayed with everything she had for her mother lying at home alone.

Dorothy rapped sharply on the healer's door. The door swung open, revealing a bewildered-looking Nancy, her shawl thrown hastily around her shoulders. "Dorothy?"

Dorothy nodded, too winded to reply, and tried not to imagine what she looked like — her cheeks red and her chestnut hair tumbling out of her *kapp* to land in a curtain around her neck that lightly brushed the top of her shoulders.

"What's wrong?" Nancy asked as she put her arm around the young woman's shoulders and ushered her into the house.

"My mother," Dorothy wheezed as she clamped her hand harder against the pain in her side.

"Your *mamm?*" Saul, Nancy's son, walked into the living room.

Saul was tall and lean, with blue eyes, blonde hair, and a quick wit. Dorothy surveyed him through her lashes as Nancy directed her to one of the couches. On a good day, Dorothy couldn't deny Saul was handsome, and now was no exception —especially with his hair rumpled and a hammer clenched loosely in his hand. But now was not the time to be surveying him. "Is everything all right?" he asked.

Nancy shook her head. "I'm not sure what's going on yet, but could you please get this poor young woman a glass of water?"

Dorothy tried to stop them from doing anything except listen to her. They were wasting precious time as her mother lay in pain, but she still couldn't do much more than shallow, rapid breathing. Out of the corner of her eye, she saw Saul disappear and then reappear just as quickly.

"Here," Nancy said gently as she pressed a cool glass of water into Dorothy's hand. "Drink that, and then tell us what's wrong."

Dorothy drained the entire glass in a few gulps before handing it back to Nancy, who gestured for Saul to refill it. He disappeared briefly before reappearing and passing another full glass to his mother.

"Now you've caught your breath," Nancy said as she handed the full glass to Dorothy once again. "Please tell us what's the matter."

"My mother," Dorothy immediately blurted. "She's not well."

"Can you tell me some of her symptoms?"

Dorothy nodded. "She's currently lying on the couch with a cold compress pressed to her forehead, in so much pain there are tears constantly streaming down her cheeks."

Nancy and Saul exchanged looks.

"Sounds like it could be a migraine," the healer murmured as she started moving around the room, collecting various herbal remedies. "Have you seen any other symptoms previously?"

Dorothy nodded as she finished off the water in her glass. "She's been eating less and less, walking around like she's in pain, forgetting things, sensitive to light..."

"Okay," Nancy put another item into her leather satchel before turning to her son. "Saul, we're going to need your help."

"I'll bring the horse and buggy around. Bernice clearly can't wait until you two get there on foot. Just give me a minute."

Dorothy couldn't help but feel a sense of gratitude for the Beachey family. They had always been kind to her and her family, and now they were rushing to help her sick mother.

When Dorothy's father had suffered his accident—Dorothy didn't remember much as she'd been only an infant of two years when it happened—Nancy had tried everything in her power to help him. However, there was nothing she or any of the *Englisch* doctors could do to save his life.

Dorothy felt a pang of guilt as she thought about her mother lying at home, in pain and alone. She wished she hadn't had to leave her even for this bit of time, but she knew Nancy was the only one who could help, and no one else could have alerted the healer of her mother's distress.

Dorothy blindly followed Nancy out of the house, her mind racing too fast about her mother's condition to notice her surroundings. She knew Nancy was the best healer in the county, but she couldn't help worrying about what would happen if all her herbs and natural remedies couldn't help her mother.

It didn't take long for Saul to drive the buggy around, and the two women climbed in. As they traveled through the twilight settling on the countryside, the wagon was silent as Dorothy's thoughts remained on her mother. She remembered how Bernice would sing to her when she was little to help soothe her to sleep and keep the nightmares at bay. Dorothy also fondly remembered how her mother would tuck her in at night, no matter how difficult her day had been beforehand. There was no denying Bernice had done her best, yet she always seemed so tired without having Dorothy's father around to help.

The longer she thought about it, the more Dorothy couldn't bear thinking about losing her mother, not when Bernice still had so much life left to live. She still didn't want to believe there was anything wrong with Bernice, but the way she'd been lying there, so weak on the couch, she knew there was.

Finally, after what felt like hours, they arrived at Dorothy's house. Nancy wasted no time rushing into the house and kneeling at Bernice's side before taking her pulse and murmuring questions. As the healer worked, Dorothy could see the concern etched on her face.

For what seemed to be an eternity, Nancy worked to ease her mother's pain, applying compresses and administering various herbal remedies. And finally, Bernice's breathing grew steady, and her face relaxed.

Dorothy sighed in relief as she watched her mother, an expression of peace on her face instead of the usual discomfort.

As she sat at her mother's side and took her hand, Dorothy knew a long road of recovery was ahead, but she was grateful that her mother rested comfortably for now. She listened to her mother's breathing and knew she had Nancy and Saul to thank for it.

Chapter Three

Beatrice squinted as her eyes opened a crack. She could see blurry figures around her, but focusing on their worried faces took a few moments.

The first person to come into focus was a distraught Dorothy. Tears slowly traced down her cheeks, and her hands were clasped so firmly around one of Bernice's hands that the older woman's fingers were numb.

The remaining two faces were those of Saul and Nancy Beachey, and Bernice knew precisely why they were there.

"Dorothy," Bernice admonished weakly as she turned her head toward her daughter, "I thought I told you not to get Nancy. Didn't I tell you I was fine?"

Dorothy shook her head rapidly from side to side. "I had to disobey you for the first time in my life. You looked like you were in terrible pain, and how you were lying there scared me. So I ran to get Nancy's help."

"You ... *ran* all the way to Nancy's house?"

Dorothy nodded. "I did."

"Well done," Bernice replied, weak but still sounding impressed. "We don't need a horse to pull the buggy anymore."

Everyone's eyebrows rose at the sound of her joke in such a solemn and tense situation.

Nancy chuckled a little. "I need you two youngsters to go and fetch some firewood. Otherwise, all our hard work will have been for nothing," the healer instructed gently once her mirth had subsided.

Dorothy opened her mouth as if to argue, but Bernice squeezed her fingers as hard as she could. It felt to Dorothy like her mother was barely even tensing her fingers; her grip was so weak. "Go, *liebchen*. I'll be fine."

Dorothy nodded reluctantly before she got to her feet and followed Saul outside. She couldn't trust herself to say anything without bursting into awful, encompassing sobs.

. . .

Once outside, the warm evening air cocooned Dorothy like a breezy hug. Saul was close on her heels and immediately set out to do the task given to them. "I hope *Mamm* is going to be okay," she finally said.

Saul didn't reply as he gathered suitable wood to add to the wood box. He'd likely seen cases like Bernice's before, as he often helped his mother on calls, especially when he was younger. Dorothy wondered whether he'd ever seen someone in such pain with a good diagnosis before, and maybe he didn't want to say anything and potentially upset her.

"She's going to be okay, *ain't so?*" Dorothy pressed as she threw her arms out helplessly, talking more to herself than anyone else. Saul let her speak into the warm evening air, knowing that venting feelings and not caring who was listening was much better than keeping things bottled up.

It took about five minutes before Saul gathered as much wood as he could hold. He turned toward the house again, only realizing then that his surroundings were eerily quiet. Dorothy had gone silent and disappeared from his line of sight at some point without him noticing.

"I think I have enough wood," Saul said, but he immediately turned around at the slight sound Dorothy made behind him.

Dorothy was sitting in the dirt at the base of one of the trees, her skirts pooled at her feet. She was leaning her back against the trunk with her face buried in her arms, which were folded on top of her knees.

"Dorothy?" he queried quietly as he set the wood down nearby and walked hesitantly toward her.

"What will I do if this is more serious than she makes it out to be?" Dorothy whispered in a raw voice, breaking Saul's heart. He couldn't begin to imagine what Dorothy was going through; he didn't even want to entertain the thought of losing his own mother.

"You'll be all right," he eventually answered as he shuffled awkwardly from foot to foot and rubbed the back of his neck.

Dorothy shrugged before her shoulders started shaking as fresh sobs wracked her body. "I don't know if I will," she choked out between tears.

Saul crouched down in front of her. He wished he could touch her, hold her hand, and give her some human contact, but he knew that would be too forward. He hated feeling this helpless. "The Lord doesn't give us anything we can't handle," he said gently after a few seconds of hesitation.

"I don't know if that's quite true," Dorothy replied with a soft, sad laugh that sounded more like another sob than anything else. "It doesn't feel like it right now."

"Trust Him," Saul replied passionately. "And if not Him at this moment, trust me."

Dorothy's head shot up, and she looked at Saul like she'd never seen him before. She recalled what she felt the few times he'd asked to court her in the past. Her heart had fluttered, and she'd desperately wanted to say yes, but her loyalty to her mother and the fear of losing him like she had her father, prevailed.

Saul's eyes held a new softness Dorothy had never seen before, and she found herself drawn to him in a way she couldn't explain. She wondered what it would be like to surrender to her curiosity and ignore her fears while finally agreeing to court him. She'd been thinking about what it would be like since he'd first asked her out, but the overwhelming fear of ending up as miserable as her mother paralyzed her every time.

Saul noticed the change in Dorothy's expression, and his heart raced. He had always been attracted to her and had asked to court her more than once. She'd turned him down every time, but he knew she had her own reasons, which he respected. Still, he prayed every night that she'd say yes. And now, as he looked into her eyes, he felt overwhelmed with the feeling that he needed to say something.

"Dorothy, I know we've talked about this before, and this is not the best time, but I have to ask you again," he said, his voice barely above a whisper. "When this is all over and your *mamm* is better... will you consider courting?"

"I ... don't know, Saul," Dorothy said, a frown creasing above her beautiful eyes. Her expression was closed off, and her voice was still thick with tears. "Now is definitely not the best time to ask me about this. I'm worried about *Mamm*, and I have my own ... concerns with courting, which you'll probably never understand..." Dorothy looked toward the house and dashed the tears from her cheeks as she tried to regulate her breathing.

Saul nodded and apologized, understanding Dorothy's words and hesitation.

"Take all the time you need," he said, standing up and walking back toward the small wood pile. "But know I'm here for you, no matter what."

Dorothy slowly stood up and brushed the dirt off her dress, feeling embarrassed and confused by her feelings. On the one hand, she felt guilty about seriously considering Saul's request while her mother was ill only a few feet away. But on the other hand, Dorothy knew Beatrice would be encouraging her to follow her heart if she was in the right frame of mind. But then again, if something happened to Saul, Dorothy didn't want to be pining for him the rest of her life like Beatrice had continually pined for her father.

Dorothy felt like her head would explode with all the thoughts and worries running through it.

"I should go check on *Mamm*," she said. She retrieved the small pile of wood she'd gathered before losing her composure and started walking toward the house.

Saul nodded, knowing that Bernice's health was the most important thing to focus on at that moment. He picked up the wood he'd collected and followed Dorothy back to the house.

As they entered the front room, they found Bernice lying on the couch, still looking weak, while Nancy sat beside her.

The second Dorothy and Saul had been out of earshot and the front door closed behind them, Nancy had sat down at Bernice's side. "Bernice," the healer said gently but firmly. "Do you have anything you want to tell me?"

Bernice turned her head away from Nancy, and tears leaked, unbidden, from under her closed eyelids. "*Nee.* I can't...."

"Bernice," Nancy said gently. "I know there's something, and I have my suspicions, but I need to know. I need you to tell me."

Bernice sighed and nodded weakly but didn't say anything, though a frown creased her brow.

"What is it?" Nancy asked again as she squeezed the sick woman's fingers in her own.

Bernice took a deep, shaky breath. She hesitated momentarily before finally revealing her secret, "I likely have a brain tumor." Her shoulders sank even further into the cushions, but she felt relief just the same. She didn't realize how good sharing her burden with someone would feel.

Nancy's eyes widened. "*What?* Bernice, have you gone to see someone?"

"I realized there was a problem with my brain when I started forgetting simple things, like how to clean the floors or sew or my daughter's name. So, I went to an *Englisch* doctor on one of the days Mrs. Fisher canceled on me." Bernice took in Nancy's shocked expression, "I know, I know. I shouldn't have done it in secret, and the Lord knows I'm still paying off the bills. But the doctor... he confirmed my suspicions that something was terribly wrong."

"You can get treatment," Nancy began before the sick woman interrupted.

"I have refused all the treatment available and further testing because I can't afford it." As weak as she'd sounded before, Bernice's sentence was firm and uncompromising.

"But the—"

"I know the district will help me pay the bills, if not pay them off completely for me, but they already support Dorothy and me so much that I couldn't think of asking for more money. Not to mention, even though he received *Englisch* medicine, it still didn't save my John..."

"Your husband fell off a roof during a barn raising. It's hardly the same thing. No medicine, whether traditional or *Englisch*, would've healed his injuries after such a fall," Nancy replied firmly.

Beatrice nodded. "I'm aware. I'm too far gone anyway now. Treatments would only ... prolong what's going to happen anyway."

There were a few moments of silence before Nancy started talking again.

"Bernice..." the healer began awkwardly.

"*Jah?*"

"You know you have to tell her."

"Dorothy?"

Nancy nodded firmly.

"The last thing I want to do is burden her with my health."

Nancy shook her head, her expression tight. "Your daughter has watched you decline," the healer began." She's already noticed things aren't right with you. In fact, she told me about your symptoms, clearly from keen observation, as you stubbornly refused to ask for any help or divulge whatever you were going through. I thought you had a migraine, but the more she went on, the more I realized it was something more serious."

Bernice sighed like the weight of the world was back on her shoulders. "I can't," she eventually replied in a broken whisper. "How do you tell your only child you're dying from something growing in your brain?"

"You *can*," Nancy said; her heart was aching seeing her friend in such torment. She lifted the ailing woman's hand and pressed it to Bernice's rapidly fluttering heart. "In fact, you *must*."

Bernice opened her mouth to argue, but before the women could discuss anything further, Dorothy and Saul walked in, their arms full of wood.

"Is everything all right?" Dorothy immediately asked as she took in her mother, looking upset, with Nancy holding their hands to Bernice's heart.

"*Jah*, we've been talking," Nancy replied. "I was checking your mother's heart rate."

"And?" Dorothy asked anxiously as she put the wood aside and hurried again to her mother's side.

Saul silently walked over to the wood box and put his pile inside before doubling back and picking up Dorothy's discarded logs.

"Your mother has a bit of an elevated heart rate, but that's not unexpected given the circumstances," Nancy reassured the young woman. "What she needs right now is some rest, and maybe some fluids if you can encourage her to have some. Unfortunately, my remedy for her pain won't help for very long. It's a temporary relief, I'm afraid." The healer gently squeezed Dorothy's shoulder as she walked past her before gathering her medical supplies.

"Well, then, what will help?" Dorothy demanded, her tone climbing.

"Your mother needs to talk to you," Nancy replied firmly as she fixed Bernice with a look that Dorothy wasn't even going to try to decipher. "Saul, will you light the fire for them, please? Then we need to get going. It's near dark, and I don't want to be on the road too late at night."

"Thank you for taking care of me," Bernice said, her voice still weak as Dorothy took up vigil beside her mother's bedside and resumed holding the older woman's hand.

"It's what I do," Nancy replied. "Remember what I told you. And Dorothy," the healer continued as she walked toward the front door, her bag of remedies clutched in her hand, "if you need anything, anything at all, please don't hesitate to come again to fetch me."

Dorothy nodded and felt herself tearing up again. "Thank you," she said in a choked whisper as mother and son took their leave.

"Dorothy," Bernice sighed tiredly once they were alone, "I have something I have to tell you, *liebchen.*"

Chapter Four

Dorothy saw the tears in her mother's eyes. Her heart sank. She knew what was coming but didn't want to hear or accept it.

"What is it, *Mamm?*" she asked, her voice barely above a whisper.

Bernice took a deep breath. "I recently went to see an *Englisch* doctor without telling you," she said, her voice trembling with every word. "I'd noticed things beforehand, like how I was struggling to see and walk and even remember your name. Everything was too bright and loud, and I couldn't remember the last time I wanted to eat something without feeling nauseous at the thought." Bernice hesitated, clearly gathering her strength before she continued. "The doctor says I likely have a brain tumor."

Dorothy felt like Bernice had knocked the wind out of her with those few simple words. She'd suspected something was wrong, but she could never have imagined something as serious as this. Tears pricked the corners of her eyes, but she forced them back so she could speak coherently.

"*Ach, Mamm*," she said, her voice breaking as much as she resisted her impending tears. "Why didn't you tell me as soon as you knew? Or at least sooner than now?"

"I didn't want to worry you, *liebchen*," Bernice said, her voice barely above a whisper. "And ... I can't afford the treatment. And I will not burden the district with the bills."

"But we *have* to get treatment," Dorothy insisted as her heart shattered. Her mother had always been strong and independent if a little downtrodden. But now, she was facing a battle she didn't even want to try and win.

Bernice shook her head before wincing from the sudden movement. "*Nee*. We don't have the money for it, and I'm well beyond treatment now. I want to spend the rest of my time here with you as I await reuniting with *Gott* and my beloved John."

"*Mamm*," Dorothy said, her voice filled with emotion. "We'll find a way. We'll figure something out. We'll sell the house, or we'll...we'll..." Dorothy trailed off as her voice broke, and the tears she'd been putting off came over her in a wave.

Bernice shook her head, cutting her off. "*Nee*, Dorothy," she said firmly. "I've made up my mind. I won't put us in debt for something that won't work. I've been waiting for so long to be with John again. I know I'm leaving you behind, but ... I want you to promise me something."

Dorothy looked up at her mother, tears streaming down her face. "Anything, *Mamm*."

"I want you to promise me you'll be strong," Bernice said, her voice barely above a whisper. "You'll care for yourself and not let this tear you apart. Find yourself a *gut* man, settle down, and make me happy. You're the only family I have left. And ... I need to know you'll be okay and have the big family I always wanted but could never have."

Dorothy nodded, her throat tight with emotion. "I-I promise, *Mamm*," she said, her voice barely above a whisper. "I'll be strong. I'll have a big family. For you."

Bernice smiled weakly at her daughter, and Dorothy leaned forward to give her mother the gentlest of hugs.

As they held each other, Dorothy's eyes closed as she fought against the burn of yet more tears threatening to fall. For some reason, she couldn't shrug off the thought that it would be one of the last times she'd ever be able to hug her mother.

Dorothy stayed up the entire night at her mother's side, sponging the older woman's forehead when the pain got too great and coaxing Bernice to have a bit of water every now and then.

They spoke about many things during Bernice's waking moments, but the most recurring theme was the older woman insisting Dorothy find someone to settle down with. And as often as Dorothy brought up the subject, Bernice kept emphasizing that she wasn't interested in treatment. She wanted to live out her remaining days in peace and spend her time with Dorothy.

As much as it shattered her heart, Dorothy had no choice but to respect her mother's wishes. And by the time the morning light started to stain the sky with pastel orange, pink, and purple hues, Dorothy realized she'd begun praying for the salvation of her mother's soul.

Dorothy could hardly believe how quickly her mother's health deteriorated after the night of the headache. It was like the older woman had given up and wanted to let go.

It had only been two weeks since she'd revealed her diagnosis, and Bernice hadn't moved off the couch. She was barely able to speak and refused any other food or water.

Dorothy had been staying up all night, every night, watching her mother's shallow breathing and praying for a miracle, and for her mother to change her mind and accept treatment, and then for Bernice to be welcomed into heaven.

Dorothy had been praying so much, so constantly, she couldn't remember exactly what she was asking for anymore.

Nancy had been doing everything she could to help, popping in every day to help around the house or assist in any other way that was needed. She brought herbal remedies to help Bernice's pain management, made soup for both of them, and applied warm compresses to the older woman's aching body.

Saul was around too, keeping the wood box full, taking care of the horse and chickens, and seeing to any other responsibilities that had been overlooked. Dorothy would've expressed her gratitude in a different situation, but she was too preoccupied with Bernice to notice at times.

Her dear friend Moriah came, also, bringing food and trying to help Dorothy however she could. Dorothy appreciated her friend's presence and always felt a bit better while she was there.

Bernice was experiencing too much pain, and Dorothy could see her mother was struggling. It was the most challenging thing she'd ever had to watch, and with every passing day, she prayed to God with every fiber of her being for something more she could do to ease her mother's suffering.

One evening, two days later, while Dorothy pressed a fresh cold compress to her mother's forehead, she heard a soft whisper from Bernice.

"I love you, *liebchen*. John...." she murmured fitfully before drifting back into unconsciousness. Dorothy didn't know it then, but it was the last time her mother would speak.

The following morning, Dorothy lifted her head from where she'd fallen asleep on her mother's mattress to find Bernice's hand ice-cold in her own.

"*Mamm?*" Dorothy asked stupidly, unable to comprehend what she was feeling. "*Mamm*, wake up. Please wake up. You must wake up." As reality set in, her voice trailed off as raw sobs took over her body, and she couldn't breathe, let alone talk anymore.

The unthinkable had happened.

Her mother was dead.

Chapter Five

Dorothy was both relieved and heartbroken.

She was more relieved than she'd ever been in her life that her mother was no longer in pain, but she was so emotionally distressed that Bernice was gone, her heart physically ached. It was like someone was pulling her heart from her chest.

Hand-in-hand with her overwhelming grief, Dorothy felt anger that her mother had kept her illness a secret for so long, leaving her with hardly any time to prepare for her death and no time to convince her to get treatment.

"I can't believe she didn't tell me sooner," Dorothy sobbed a few hours later when Nancy arrived and the necessary procedures to give her mother a proper send-off had begun. "I had no time to prepare."

"Oh, *liebchen*," Nancy sighed as she rocked Dorothy to and fro in a hug. Dorothy had sunk to the floor in Nancy's arms as soon as the healer had embraced her, and all the emotions she'd been keeping at bay overflowed. "You never have time to prepare for the death of a loved one." She kissed the top of the distraught young woman's *kapp* and held her as she cried.

In the following blur of days, Nancy and Saul were a tremendous help to Dorothy. They helped her with all the details that needed seeing to, even ensuring Dorothy ate something regularly.

Saul was incredibly supportive, quietly doing whatever needed to be done without imposing on Dorothy's grief. He chopped wood, fixed fences, and cared for the animals. Whatever job he saw needed to be done, no matter how big or small, he did it without Dorothy asking.

The community rallied together to help prepare for Bernice's viewing and the funeral. Moriah spent the first two nights with her, sleeping in the next room. Dorothy did little more than toss and turn, but she was grateful for her friend's presence, nonetheless.

Dorothy had never planned a funeral before and didn't know where to begin. Thankfully, the other women in the district, Nancy included, took charge, offering their guidance and support every step of the way. They took it upon themselves to ensure that Bernice was properly dressed in her wedding dress, as was their tradition. It was a tearful time, for many of the folks had engaged Bernice regularly to clean their houses or help in other ways. And Bernice had sold them delicious baked goods and looked after their children. Dorothy was acutely aware this was done to help her mother and her financially, and it touched her heart that her mother was so esteemed.

When Dorothy saw her mother in her coffin through her welling tears, Bernice looked more at peace than she ever had during her waking life. It gave Dorothy hope that she was in a much better place, reunited with the father Dorothy could barely remember.

The district women also ensured that Dorothy's house was clean and comfortable, with plenty of chairs for the mourners who would come to pay their respects.

Even though it was the middle of summer, the day of Bernice's burial dawned overcast and grey. There was no rain, save for a short drizzle here and there, but it was the appropriate weather to reflect the mood of the mourners at the funeral.

People, nearly the entire district, arrived at her house in droves, bringing with them food and their heartfelt condolences. Some had known Bernice since childhood, while others had only met her in passing. Some were the children Bernice had looked after over the previous years. Regardless, the entire community felt a profound loss at her death, and the entirety of the Rock Point Amish community seemed to be there to pay their respects.

Dorothy greeted each visitor as they arrived, her heart heavy with grief. She tried to stay strong, but the tears came unbidden, and she continued to wipe them away.

After the burial, the mourners gathered in the front room of Dorothy's house for a meal. The other women in the district had prepared the food, which was abundant and delicious, not that Dorothy was particularly hungry. They had made everything from casseroles to cakes, and there was enough food to feed the entire town and then some. Dorothy sat, surrounded by her friends, but she felt alone in her overwhelming grief.

What was she going to do now?

Who would dry her tears and tell her everything would be all right?

What now?

In the background, there throughout the entire process, Saul was quietly helping wherever he could. He didn't ask for instructions or direction; he simply did what needed to be done. Dorothy didn't ask him to do any of the things he took care of, but she was more grateful for his presence than she could ever put into words. He sat close to her at the table, a comforting, steady presence amid all the chaos. He didn't say much, but his being close by was enough to ease some of Dorothy's pain. He even helped carry the dirty dishes to the kitchen, so Dorothy didn't have to worry about anything.

After everyone had eaten their fill, they filed out of Dorothy's house, one by one, after giving her one last bit of condolences or some gentle words of comfort.

Moriah came up to her toward the end of the afternoon. "I can spend the night again, if you want me to," she said softly.

Dorothy took a big breath. She was exhausted. Maybe it would be better if she were alone for a while. "Thank you, but I'm all right. I think I'll sleep tonight. I'm exhausted."

"You're sure?"

Dorothy nodded. "I'm sure. But thanks. I'm going to be fine."

"All right." Moriah gave her a tight hug and then left the house with her family.

****(

District life slowly returned to normal in the following days when nothing would ever be normal for Dorothy again. The flowers wilted, the food was eaten, and the mourners had all returned to their own lives.

Dorothy missed her mother more than words could express. She struggled to come to terms with her loss. Yet she knew she was not alone. The women in the district had shown her there was still goodness in the world, even amid tragedy. And

Saul had shown her that people still cared, even in the darkest times.

Only after everyone had gone did Dorothy realize how alone she was. Moriah, Saul, and Nancy checked on her many times during the first few days, which helped. But Moriah often had to leave quickly, as her mother had just had twins and needed her help.

Dorothy always closed the door behind them, feeling the emptiness and silence of the house. There was no reassuring sound of her mother's humming; there was no oven on; there was no wash hanging outside.

There was nothing except a cold, empty house, and Dorothy sank to the floor as the reality of how alone she was filled her with despair.

Chapter Six

Through her days of grief, Dorothy had moments to sit and think about Saul, and how helpful he had been - and still was - in supporting her after her loss; she began to see Saul in a different light. She couldn't help but remember his kind eyes, his gentle demeanor, and his unwavering strength. He had always been there when she needed him but never pushed himself on her. She would be eternally grateful for that.

Dorothy realized she was getting closer to Saul, but she didn't want to overthink it. He'd been welcome company in the time directly after losing her mother, yet she didn't want to give him any hope for the future if there was none.

One day, about two weeks after the funeral, Dorothy walked down the narrow streets of Rock Point, carrying bags of groceries for food she didn't feel like making. She couldn't help but feel suffocated by the memories that lingered around every corner. The quaint town, once a source of comfort, had become a constant reminder of her mother's absence. The brick buildings and the old-fashioned lampposts she had once found charming now seemed dreary and oppressive.

Once she returned to her empty house and mindlessly started unpacking the shopping, she realized how she longed for a fresh start. She needed a chance to leave behind painful memories and find a new beginning.

And she definitely needed to find something that would bring in some money.

The following day, Dorothy decided to go for the long walk to Moriah's house. She needed the air, the activity, and some time to think about precisely what she would say to her best friend.

"Morning, Moriah," Dorothy said as she came across her best friend picking flowers by the side of the road.

"Dorothy," Moriah greeted her back as she looked up from the bouquet of daisies she was putting together. "What are you doing here?"

"I needed a walk, and it's always nice to see you."

"Well, it's lovely to see you, too," Moriah replied earnestly as she linked arms with Dorothy, making things feel like old times again, if only for a second. "I wanted to come and see you sooner, but with *Mamm* and the twins, I haven't been able to get away. This is the first time I've been able to sneak out of the house all week."

"Sounds like you need a rest," Dorothy observed mildly.

"You have no idea," Moriah replied tiredly.

"Then I have a suggestion for you." Dorothy took a deep breath, trying to steady her emotions. "I think I need to get away for a while," she said, her voice trembling slightly.

Moriah put a comforting hand on her shoulder. "What do you mean, get away?"

"I mean, leave Rock Point. It's just too hard to be here with all the memories of *Mamm*. I need a fresh start," Dorothy explained, tears welling in her eyes. "And from the sounds of things, you want to get away, too."

"Where would you want to go?" Moriah asked before something seemed to occur to her. "And *jah*, I want a little break from things, but only temporarily. You're making it sound like forever. I can't possibly do that."

"I'm not sure about the time frame," Dorothy admitted, "but everything around me is making it much harder to recover from *Mamm's* death. I need a chance to do something different."

"Nobody expects you to heal overnight," Moriah said gently.

"I know, but I'm tired of constantly being reminded of my loss," Dorothy replied, her voice shaking. "And I was thinking that maybe we could go visit Brewster, Ohio. We could hire a van and spend the day. There is a large Amish population there, and it might be a nice change of scenery and just what I need."

Moriah studied Dorothy's face before nodding. "I can try to get away. I don't know. It depends on whether *Mamm* can spare me or not." Seeing Dorothy's discouraged expression, she quickly added. "I'll do my best to come with you. But only one day. When do you want to go?"

"As soon as possible," Dorothy said, feeling a weight lifted off her shoulders, knowing that her best friend was standing with her.

Two days later, Dorothy and Moriah were on their way in a rented van. They rode through the countryside, taking in the sights. The scenery was lovely. The endless expanse of green fields that stretched out before them filled Dorothy with a sense of contentment she hadn't felt in a long while. The scent of hay mingled with the crisp, cool air, coming in the open windows rejuvenating Dorothy's spirit.

As they approached the town of Brewster, the towering silos and the horse-drawn buggies that dotted the streets brought a smile to Dorothy's face. The gentle clip-clop of the horses' hooves and the chatter of children running by were soothing, and she felt a sense of peace wash over her.

"It's a right nice town," Moriah said, gazing out the window.

Dorothy smiled, feeling a sense of excitement and anticipation building in her stomach. "I can't wait to walk around."

As soon as the driver parked the van, they got out and wandered the streets. It didn't take long before they stumbled across a bustling store filled with the Amish community's handmade goods. The aroma of fresh-baked bread mingled with the sweet fragrance of apple butter, and the intricate quilts and wooden toys were a sight to behold. The Amish children played together, laughing and giggling, their simple joy infectious. As Dorothy and Moriah explored the market, they chatted with the locals, who welcomed them.

At one point, they realized they were hungry and stopped at a small bakery stall. They bought and ate some warm, buttery pretzels, and they each had a whoopie pie.

The bustling energy of Brewster, coupled with the serene beauty of the surrounding countryside, had rekindled Dorothy's hope and filled her heart with a newfound sense of purpose. She knew that leaving Rock Point would not be easy, but with the support of Moriah and the inspiration she found in Brewster, she felt ready to embark on a new chapter in her life.

Simply put, she wanted to stay.

Moriah and Dorothy were just about to return to the van when Dorothy came across a quaint little café with a sign in the window that read, "Help Wanted."

"Moriah," Dorothy called to her friend, who was admiring a flower stall nearby, "maybe we should look at this place." She gestured behind her at the café.

Moriah looked skeptical. "Are you hungry? Wait. It says help wanted. Are you truly interested in asking about that? Do you... Are you thinking of staying?"

Dorothy hesitated for a moment before saying, "I don't know, maybe. You know I've always been interested in a café. And I could use the money. Let's just go inside and see what it's all about."

The café was a charmingly old-fashioned establishment with wooden floors, tables, and a cozy fireplace in the corner. The owner—or so it said on his name tag - was a short, balding man who greeted them warmly as they entered the place.

"Hello, there. I'm Henry Kinsberg. Shall I show you to a table?" he asked with a friendly smile.

Dorothy took a deep breath to gather her thoughts before saying, "We just saw your sign outside. Are you still looking for help?"

Henry's eyes lit up. "I am. I've been looking for some waitresses to add to the staff, but I haven't had much luck. Hmm. Are you interested? Because I have a feeling you two would be perfect."

Dorothy glanced at Moriah, who looked unsure. "I don't think we're qualified," Moriah said hesitantly.

Henry waved his hand dismissively. "Nonsense, I'm sure you'll do just fine. This is an old-fashioned café, after all. We're all about simplicity and hard work."

Dorothy felt a surge of excitement in her belly at the prospect of working in such a charming place. "*Jah*, we'd be interested. But only if we can work together," she said, hoping Moriah would agree.

Moriah appeared shocked and tugged on Dorothy's sleeve. Dorothy turned toward her. "You know I can't leave *Mamm* alone with the twins," she said under her breath.

Henry clapped his hands together. "Do you have any references? If you don't, that's all right because I've got a good feeling about you two. And I've hired Amish in the past, and they've been my very best employees. You wouldn't have to start right away. I'd give you a few days to organize things. But to add more incentive, and as part of your wages, I have a tiny apartment above the café where you can stay if you need a place. It's not much, but it's cozy and comfortable."

Dorothy and Moriah exchanged a look of disbelief. And then Dorothy saw that Moriah was beginning to look excited, too.

"Come with me. I'll show it to you," Henry continued as he gestured for them to follow him up the set of stairs behind him.

As Dorothy walked upstairs to their potential new home, she couldn't help but feel grateful for the unexpected opportunity that had brought them to this little corner of Ohio. She was beaming with barely contained excitement as she and Moriah were shown around the apartment. The prospect of a fresh start in this new town was invigorating, and she couldn't wait to see what the future held.

Moriah, on the other hand, now seemed uneasy again. "Who am I fooling? What about my mother?" she repeated. "How is she going to get along without me?"

Dorothy put a hand on her shoulder. "Just ask her. You have other sisters who can help. Just ask. This is a wonderful chance for us. And you could send most of your earnings home. We shouldn't need much to live on here. Especially with a place to live."

Moriah nodded slowly, still looking unsure but hopefully willing to give it a chance.

As they thanked Henry and returned to the van, Dorothy knew she still had a long road ahead of her to be ready for such a move, but she would face it with strength and determination for she had a very good feeling about the move.

Chapter Seven

As Dorothy and Moriah returned to Rock Point, Dorothy decided to sell her childhood home. She didn't want to hold onto any ties to the past, and the thought of returning to her old life filled her with dread. Besides, she couldn't afford to keep the place going when she wasn't even there.

"I'm going to sell the house," Dorothy announced decisively when they were halfway home.

"You're going to *what?*" Moriah asked in horror.

"I'm going to sell the house," Dorothy repeated, feeling a strange sense of peace about her decision. She squared her shoulders and raised her chin slightly. Then she smiled and looked out the window, admiring the farmhouses whizzing by.

Not everyone agreed with Dorothy. Saul and Nancy took the news of her decision in much the same way as Moriah had when they visited her after she got back. But Dorothy was determined to move forward.

Saul tried to be supportive, but his heart was breaking. He had undeniable feelings for Dorothy. If he hadn't been sure about them before, he was completely sure now. He had fallen completely in love with her while he supported her during and after her mother's death. However, he could see her mind was set on leaving. Dorothy's ambition and drive were two of the things that had always attracted him to her. So, he tried to be open and happy about her decision, but he couldn't help feeling a bit hurt. He had hoped she was beginning to fall for him, too.

"Dorothy, are you sure this is what you want?" he asked, trying to hide the frustration in his voice.

Dorothy sighed. "I have to do this, Saul. I can't keep living here. I need a fresh start, and Brewster is just what I need."

Saul nodded slowly, trying to keep his emotions in check. "I-I don't want you to regret anything. All your friends are here."

"He's right, and don't forget that. But if you must go, we send you with *Gott's* blessings," Nancy said reassuringly, reaching forward to squeeze Dorothy's wrist. "And we'll always be here if you need us for anything."

Dorothy looked at Saul for his reaction as she nodded automatically in response to Nancy's words. She felt a twinge of something she couldn't quite identify as she realized Saul was clearly upset about her decision. But she pushed it aside, knowing her focus needed to be on her new life in Brewster.

"I won't regret it, Saul. This is what I need," she said, the words sounding a bit hollow to her own ears. She raised her chin, trying to regain her confidence with her decision.

"What if an *Englischer* wants to buy your house?" Saul asked. "Will you sell it to them?"

"I don't know," she replied honestly.

Dorothy couldn't shake off her discomfort as she waved goodbye to the Beacheys a short time later. What would she do if an *Englischer* wanted to buy her house? Would it matter? Would her closest neighbors be upset with her? What would her mother say if she were here?

As much as Dorothy was now of two minds about selling her house, she was still intent on moving into the small apartment above the café. She even went so far as to take two suitcases of belongings with her to Rock Point on the bus.

She met Henry again, and he was happy to have her begin moving into the apartment. They settled on a starting day for work, and that made Dorothy excited all over again. But he clearly noticed that something was bothering her.

"What's on your mind?" he asked, after handing over the apartment key.

Dorothy hesitated for a moment before deciding to share her worries with them. "I want to sell my house in Rock Point. The memories there of my mother are... too painful right now. Yesterday, an *Englischer* expressed interest." It had been what she'd dreaded all along. "He wants to put in electricity and make it a short-term rental."

Henry's eyes widened before he thoughtfully furrowed his brow. "And how do you feel about it?"

"I-I don't know," Dorothy replied honestly. "Part of me wonders if I should hold onto the house and keep it, but mostly I want to sell it. I fear my friends and neighbors in Rock Point don't understand."

Henry nodded and scratched the back of his head. "Look, at the end of the day, you must do what's best for you, Dorothy. I'm sure your neighbors and friends will understand."

"I hope so," Dorothy replied gratefully.

"And if you do decide to sell," he continued as he took one of the suitcases Dorothy had been holding and started up the stairs, "I might know a few Amish families in that area who might be interested."

Dorothy smiled at the thought of her childhood home being cared for by a loving Amish family. "Thank you, Henry. I'll keep that in mind."

After unpacking her suitcases, Dorothy left the café feeling more at ease, knowing she had people who cared about her and her wellbeing.

The days sped past in a blur of packing and taking the bus between Rock Point and Brewster, and before long, it was the day before Dorothy and Moriah were due to move into the little apartment above the café. Dorothy had expressed fear that Moriah would change her mind and not go, but so far, Moriah had been outwardly agreeable to the move, even acting a bit excited.

At the little farewell party Saul, Nancy, and Moriah's family were throwing for them, Dorothy sat across from Moriah, her eyes shining with excitement as she spoke about their dream of someday owning the café. Moriah tried to listen, but her thoughts kept drifting back to Peter Lapp.

Since she'd started helping her mother with the twins, Moriah had been the one to bring in the milk every morning. At first, she'd walk outside and pick up the full bottles. But after meeting Peter once when he'd been running late, she'd found herself getting up earlier so she could wait to see him on his milk rounds. It didn't take long for Peter to show an interest in her. He was kind and funny and made her heart skip a beat whenever he was around. Moriah tried to push him out of her mind, but she couldn't deny her growing feelings for him.

Dorothy paused in her chatting and looked at Moriah, likely sensing something was off. "Is everything okay?" she asked, concerned.

Moriah forced a smile. "*Jah*, everything's fine. I'm just tired. The twins barely sleep through the night most of the time."

Dorothy didn't look convinced, but she didn't push the issue. Instead, she continued talking about their plans for the café. "We could help make it even more wonderful," she said. "People would come from all over just to experience the old-fashioned charm. And the food's *gut,* too. We've tasted it."

Moriah nodded automatically in agreement, but her mind continued to be elsewhere. She wondered if she would be around long enough to see their dream come true. Her feelings for Peter grew stronger every day, and she didn't know how long she could deny them.

Her thoughts were in turmoil as they walked over to the food table together. She didn't want to risk ruining her friendship with Dorothy, but she couldn't ignore her feelings for Peter. She really wanted to take a chance with him and see where it went, rather than lose out because she was moving away.

As they began filling their plates, Moriah hesitated momentarily as she gathered her thoughts before speaking. "Dorothy, can I talk to you about something? Over here?"

Dorothy turned to face her, her eyes full of concern. She followed Moriah to the corner of the room where no one would hear them. "Of course. What's on your mind?"

Moriah took a deep breath before speaking. "It's about a man. Peter Lapp. You know him. I-I think we might have feelings for each other."

Dorothy's face creased into a frown. "Wait. What are you telling me? *Ach,* do you not want to go? Why didn't you say so? Why let me think... *Ach*, why did you lie to me?"

"*Lie* to you? I—"

"*Jah*, whenever I asked what was wrong, you said you were tired. You didn't tell me your hesitation was because you'd met a man and wanted to back out of coming."

Moriah sighed heavily, feeling awful for what she had to do. "This was always more your dream than mine," she said. "I'm sorry."

Dorothy swallowed. "So, you don't want to go. That's what you're telling me."

Moriah reached forward to try and take Dorothy's hands, but Dorothy took a step back.

"I didn't think I wanted to be married," Moriah said. "I wasn't lying about that. But now, things have changed. *I* have changed. And Peter..."

Dorothy held up her hands. "Don't say anymore. I understand. I'm sad, but I understand. I'm on my own, then. I'm on my own."

Chapter Eight

"Dorothy? Are you all right?"

Dorothy's head shot up at the soft, soothing, familiar voice of Saul. Her heart skipped a beat as she turned around, hurriedly wiping her eyes.

Saul took a hesitant step toward the bench outside where she had found solace after the meal, and Dorothy forced a smile, desperately trying to push away her sadness. It seemed like she was always upset and emotional around him.

Saul repeated his question, worry etched on every line of his face. "Are you okay, Dorothy?" he asked, and his eyes searched hers.

Dorothy looked down at the ground, trying to hold back her tears. "Moriah isn't coming with me anymore," she eventually admitted, her voice barely above a whisper.

Saul took another step closer, his hand hovering near her shoulder but not touching her. He wanted to comfort her with physical touch, but he held back. "I'm sorry to hear that. Goodness, and you just found out? I'm truly sorry. Can I do anything to help?"

Dorothy shook her head. "*Nee,* I'll be okay. I-I'm sure Henry will be able to find someone else," she managed after clearing her throat.

"Are you sure about this, Dorothy? About going?" Saul asked, his voice barely above a whisper. "Moving somewhere new, where there's nobody around who knows or..." he paused for a second as he licked his lips, "...loves you?"

Dorothy looked at him, her eyes meeting his. She couldn't pretend she didn't notice his pause. "*Jah,* Saul, I'm sure. This is something I truly want to do."

Saul couldn't help but feel a pang of envy. He wanted to be the one to start over with her, to build a new life together. But he knew it was not his place to say anything.

They talked for a little while, about everything and nothing of consequence, and Saul found himself drawn to her even more, wanting to touch her, to hold her. He could feel the tension building between them, a palpable energy that was impossible to ignore, but it went against every fiber of his upbringing to act on his impulses.

At one point, their conversation came to a natural conclusion, and they ended up in companionable silence, sitting and looking out into the garden that Dorothy knew so well.

"I'm going to miss you," Saul finally said, his voice barely above a whisper.

Dorothy turned to look at him, her eyes filled with emotion. "I'm going to miss you too, Saul."

They sat there, lost in their thoughts and feelings, until Saul couldn't take it anymore. He was in love with Dorothy, but he couldn't do anything about it. He got to his feet in a sudden movement and walked a few steps away.

"Saul?"

Saul nodded, a deep frown on his face. "If you need anything, just let me know," he said softly before turning to leave.

"Saul..." Dorothy called out.

Saul turned on his heel at the sound of her voice, the concern that was on his face replaced by hope.

"*Jah?*"

Dorothy wasn't sure what to say. She had so much she wanted him to know, but she didn't know where to start.

"I'm... really looking forward to this adventure," she eventually said lamely, and as soon as Saul's expression fell, she knew it was the wrong thing to say.

"I'm sure you are," he replied.

As Dorothy watched him go, she felt a pang of regret in the pit of her stomach. She wished she could tell him how much she appreciated his friendship, how much she needed him in her life. But she couldn't, not when she had lost so much and was so focused on chasing her dream.

The next day dawned bright and early, and Dorothy was back in her hired van, heading to Brewster without Moriah. As she left Rock Point behind, she tried not to feel bitter toward Moriah or to think of Saul. However, the countryside blurring past lulled her into thinking about everything that had happened to her. From her mother dying to her dearest friend letting her down, Dorothy wondered how she managed to get up in the mornings.

"Where's Moriah?" Henry asked as Dorothy walked into the café with her last bag.

"She decided against coming," Dorothy replied, her tone clear that she didn't want to talk about it.

Henry's mouth opened and then shut again before he moved out of the way so Dorothy could go up to the apartment.

Even he could pick up on her foul mood.

"I'll work extra hard to cover for the lack of Moriah," Dorothy said from the top of the stairs.

"And I'll be on the lookout for someone to fill her spot," Henry replied, "It's a pity, you two were perfect together."

"I know."

Days turned into weeks, and Dorothy threw herself into her work. She was always busy, always on the move. Working at the café kept her on her toes and distracted her like nothing else had in Rock Point. But every now and then, when the café was empty and she was alone with her thoughts, she couldn't help but wonder what could have been.

One evening, as Dorothy was closing the café, she was shocked to have Saul come by.

"Hello, Dorothy," he said, his voice soft, as if he didn't want to scare her off. "I-I just wanted to see how you're doing."

Dorothy turned to face him, and for a moment, they just stood there, looking into each other's eyes. The air between them was charged with tension. Dorothy broke the spell when she almost dropped one of the chairs she was stacking on a table.

"H-Hello, Saul. I-I'm doing fine." Her voice sounded calm, but inside she was doing the jig. Dorothy realized she missed him. "What in the world are you doing here? I-I can't believe I'm looking at you."

Saul stepped closer and picked up a chair to help her stack them. "I've been thinking about you a lot lately," he admitted. "And I know we've always been just friends, but I can't help wondering...what if there's something more between us? I hope... Well, maybe things have intensified since..." Saul trailed off, not wanting to bring up any painful memories.

Dorothy's heart skipped a beat. She'd thought about it too, when she was alone in her apartment after her shift ended, but she knew a romantic relationship was not possible at that moment. How could it be? They lived hours away from one another.

"I-I'm sorry Saul. I don't see how it could work. I'm so busy and... " She gestured to the café behind her.

Saul nodded, looking down at the floor. "I know. I just had to come and see you. It had to be said. I can't keep pretending I don't feel this way."

Dorothy reached out, her hand hovering above his arm, the closest she would get to touching him. "The timing isn't right." But when *would* the timing be right? What was the matter with her? She was crazy about the man. And then the image of her mother's face filled her mind. And she heard again, her mother lamenting over her long dead husband.

Saul looked at her with a sad smile. "All right, Dorothy. But I'll always be here for you, no matter what."

Dorothy felt a rush of affection for him. How she wished things could be different, but she knew she wasn't yet ready to give Saul what he was asking for. She smiled back at him, grateful for his friendship. "Thank you, Saul. I appreciate that."

"I should go," Saul said, his voice thick with emotion. "I won't be staying."

Dorothy nodded, her own voice barely above a whisper. "Thank you for coming," she said, and Saul could hear the unspoken words in her tone: "Thank you for being here for me."

He tilted his head and shoved his hands deep in his pockets, and walked toward the driver he'd hired who was standing nearby.

As Saul climbed back into the car, he couldn't help but wonder what it would be like to hold Dorothy in his arms.

For her part, Dorothy was equally conflicted. She couldn't deny the attraction she felt toward Saul, but she knew she wouldn't act on it. As she watched Saul ride away, she couldn't help but feel a sense of longing. She missed her mother, she missed Rock Point, and she missed the life she had before. But she had a good life in Brewster, and she loved working in the café just as much as she had known she would.

Chapter Nine

That evening, Dorothy sat alone in her tiny apartment, surrounded by the dim light of the setting sun coming through the front window. She had finished her shift in the café after Saul left and was feeling exhausted, but restless. She loved the work, loved the customers, and loved the thrill of helping a business run smoothly, but she couldn't shake the feeling of loneliness that seemed to permeate everything around her.

As she sat there, she remembered a stack of letters she had received earlier that day. Letters were one of the things that seemed to bring her comfort these days. She reached for them, plucked the pile from her kitchen counter, opened the first envelope, and started reading. As she read, she couldn't help but smile. The letter was from Moriah and her words were warm, filled with love and sincerity, and most of all, they were apologetic.

Dear Dorothy,

I'm sorry for everything. I'm sorry for not being there for you, for not taking the café seriously, and for not being the friend you deserve.

Please forgive me.

P.S. Peter asked me to marry him, and I agreed!

Dorothy felt a lump form in her throat as she read the words. She had been so hurt and upset when Moriah refused to move with her, but now, with the distance between them, she could see things more clearly. Moriah was happy with her life and happy with Peter, and she had no real desire to run a café. Dorothy realized she had been so caught up in her own dreams that she had assumed Moriah felt the same.

She took a deep breath and found some paper and a pen. It took her a few minutes to decide what to say before she began to write,

My dearest Moriah,

Of course, I forgive you. You are my best friend, and I love you no matter what. I'm so glad you found what makes you happy, and I hope you and Peter have a wonderful life together. As for me, the café is everything I ever wanted, and I'm so grateful for this opportunity.

Love, always,

Dorothy

As she finished the letter and folded it up, she felt a sense of peace wash over her. Maybe, just maybe, she could find lasting happiness here in Brewster, even if it meant being alone for a while. She put the letter in an envelope, addressed it, and sealed it up, ready to be posted the next day.

Dorothy then moved onto the next few letters in the pile, which were various advertisements and bills, before the last envelope, written in handwriting she didn't recognize. She opened the envelope slowly, unsure of what she would find inside.

Dear Dorothy,

I hope this letter finds you well. I've been thinking of you often since you left Rock Point. I miss our talks and walks along the lake. I wanted to let you know I'll be visiting Brewster soon. I was hoping we could meet up and catch up on old times.

Yours truly,

Saul

Dorothy felt as if she could hear Saul talking to her as she read his letter. So that explained why he'd been in town and had come to see her. Dorothy felt a rush of excitement and nervousness, hoping she might see him again, before she reminded herself that she'd successfully put a stop to anymore visits. She paced back and forth in the small room, wondering what to do. Had she done the right thing, turning him down earlier?

After a few moments of contemplation, she picked up a pen and began to write a response:

Dear Saul,

It's gut *to hear from you. I enjoyed seeing you. It was such a surprise.*

You're always welcome to stop by for a cup of coffee and a chat.

Sincerely,

Dorothy

She sealed the letter and placed it on the windowsill on top of her reply to Moriah to be mailed the next day. It had started to rain outside, and after finishing a cup of tea, Dorothy curled up on her small bed. As much as she tried to go to sleep, her thoughts would not stop swirling around and around in her head. Eventually, she managed to drift off into a fitful sleep, lulled by the steady pitter-patter of rain on the roof.

Before she knew it, Dorothy had been working at the café for three months. Her time as a waitress had flown by, and she couldn't believe how quickly she'd settled into the ritual of things. She'd ended up accepting an offer on her house from an Amish family after the *Englischer* had taken back his offer.

At first, Dorothy had been disappointed when the first deal hadn't gone through, but then she was happy when it finally went into contract with an Amish family. In truth, that was what she'd wanted all along.

Dorothy sat at one of the empty café tables, staring at the blank sheet of paper in front of her. It was a Monday evening, one of the slowest times during the week, so she'd decided to catch up on her mail while waiting for customers. She'd been trying to write a letter to Saul for hours, but her mind was foggy with exhaustion after another long day of work. She sighed and leaned back in her chair, rubbing her tired eyes.

As she sat there, her thoughts drifted to Saul. They'd been writing to each other for a couple months now, and she was surprised at how much she enjoyed their conversations. She found herself looking forward to receiving his letters and reading about his life back home on his farm.

Moriah's letters also kept her updated what was going on in her life. She was planning her wedding to Peter (and of course Dorothy was invited) and her twin brothers were growing up way too quickly.

Dorothy smiled and sometimes laughed when she read the letters her friends sent her, but she couldn't deny the feelings of longing that settled over her. As strange as it was, she missed life in Rock Point.

The bell above the café door jingled, pulling Dorothy out of her thoughts, and she jumped up, startled. It took her a second, but she soon recognized Saul standing in the doorway, with a big smile on his face.

"Saul," she exclaimed, rushing over to him. "What a lovely surprise."

Saul chuckled at her excitement. "I was ... in the area and thought I'd stop by. I hope you don't mind. You did offer a cup of coffee and a chat whenever I was here, if I recall."

"Of course, I recall," she said, beaming at him. "I'm so glad to see you."

Saul sat down at one of the empty tables while Dorothy fixed a cup of coffee for the both of them. They caught up on each other's lives, expanding on some of the things that were mentioned in their letters, or chatting about something new. At one point, Saul asked more about the café and listened intently as Dorothy told him all about it. She was surprised at how genuinely interested he seemed.

"You know," he said with a grin, "I could see myself becoming a café man."

Dorothy laughed as she thought he was joking. "Oh, I don't know about that. You seem happy on the farm."

He shrugged. "Farming has its moments, but I've always been interested in food and cooking. And I'd love to work with you."

Dorothy felt a flutter in her chest at the thought of working alongside Saul. She quickly brushed it aside. He was surely joking.

Too soon after he arrived, he had to leave, and Dorothy tried to ignore the pang of sadness she felt in her stomach as he stood. He leaned in and whispered, "I'll keep dreaming of becoming a café man," before doffing his hat at her with a wink and a mischievous smile. He disappeared out the door, leaving the sound of jingling in his wake.

Dorothy smiled and watched him walk down the street, her mind swirling, like it had been a lot lately, with thoughts of what could be.

A few days after Saul visited Dorothy, Henry became ill. Dorothy was worried when she heard about it from the cook. She felt confident in keeping the café running while he was out, but the fear and anxiety of possibly losing another person she cared for were overwhelming. She knew she was likely exaggerating things, but all she could think about was how quickly her mother had gone downhill before dying.

Later that day she stepped into the café from the kitchen and was surprised to see Henry sitting at one of the empty tables, looking pale and weak.

"Dorothy," Henry said weakly, "I need your help. I need you to manage the café while I recover."

"Of course. Of course, I will. I'm happy to. You shouldn't even be out and about. You need to go back home. How are you feeling?" She hurried toward her boss. Flashbacks of holding her mother's hand as Bernice slowly faded away came to the forefront of her mind, and she pushed back the tears she could feel burning her eyes.

"It isn't so bad," Henry replied with an airy wave of his hand before he coughed. It sounded wet and sore.

"Are you sure?"

Henry nodded as he wiped his mouth with a handkerchief. "It's just a bug that's going around. But I need to know if you can take care of the place while I get better. Then I'll go home. I promise."

Dorothy had never managed the café on her own before, but she was sure she could do it. "I will do it. Are you sure you don't need me to call a doctor?" she asked, concern etched on her face.

"Naw, I just need some rest," Henry assured her. "I trust you, and I know you can run things without me."

Dorothy listened to his last-minute instructions regarding managing the café, and then he bid her farewell and left. The next few days were a blur of activity and exhaustion as she learnt on her feet. Dorothy was juggling everything from ordering supplies to scheduling staff, all while trying to keep the customers happy.

Despite the long hours and stress, Dorothy found herself dreaming of Saul. She couldn't help but imagine how wonderful it would be if he were there with her, helping to manage the café. She wondered if his offer to become a "café man" was him just showing her interest and kindness, or if he was serious about it. Dorothy had grown to care for him deeply through their letters, and the thought of him being by her side made her happy.

Dorothy only had to take care of the café on her own for a bit more than a week, and once Henry returned, he was impressed with how she had managed everything. As a result, he began to give her more responsibilities. Before Dorothy knew it, she oversaw ordering supplies and managing the staff even though Henry was well.

Chapter Ten

As much as Dorothy adored working at the café during the day, she always felt a sense of emptiness and longing as she looked around her small apartment after her workday was over. While she couldn't deny it was cozy and comfortable, it was far from being a home. Dorothy wanted a place where she could put down roots and make memories. She had been feeling especially melancholic recently, after she'd signed the final papers on the sale of her house.

She tried to shake off her feelings and focus on the present. After all, she was helping to run a successful business, and that should be enough. But as the days flew by, she found herself yearning for something more.

One evening, as she was closing the café, she saw a family walking by on the sidewalk. The parents were holding hands, and the children skipped ahead, laughing, and playing. Dorothy's heart ached at the sight of them. She was surprised as she realized she was wishing for a family of her own.

As she climbed the stairs to her apartment, Dorothy thought about her mother and how much she missed her. While they'd had their disagreements, they had been a close family of two. As Dorothy mechanically started making herself dinner, she wondered what it would be like to have someone to come home to, someone to share her life with.

When Dorothy finished her dinner, she sat at her tiny desk, crammed beside her bed, and wrote a letter to Saul. She told him how much she enjoyed his letters and how much she wished he were with her. She admitted feeling lonely and that she longed for a sense of family. She hesitated before signing her name at the end of the letter, wondering if she had said too much. But then she reminded herself that Saul had always been a good friend and a kind listener.

Dorothy kept herself busy with work. But the ache in her heart stubbornly wouldn't go away. She constantly longed for a place to call home, a family to call her own, and it only got worse as the days went by. At one point, she wondered if she would ever find what she was looking for. She also was confused and hurt that Saul hadn't responded to her letter about being lonely. It wasn't like him to stay quiet.

Dorothy took a deep breath, pulling herself out of her circular thoughts and stepped back into the bustling kitchen, determined to feel energized and ready for whatever the day held. She picked up her notepad and headed back out to the dining area, where the customers were starting to trickle in for the lunch rush.

She loved interacting with the customers, getting to know them, and making sure they had a pleasant dining experience. She made small talk with an elderly couple celebrating their anniversary and made sure to put a candle in their dessert. She chatted with a group of friends who had come in for their weekly lunch date and remembered their usual orders without having to write them down.

Before long, the café was humming with activity, and Dorothy was in her happy spot, moving around quickly and efficiently, delivering plates of steaming food to hungry customers. She felt a sense of pride in her work and in the café. She caught a glimpse of herself in the mirror and saw that her hair was a mess, a few strands tumbling out from beneath her *kapp* and there was a food stain on her apron, but she didn't care. She was happy doing what she loved, and that was all that mattered.

As the lunch rush wound down, Dorothy took a moment to catch her breath and wipe down the empty tables. As she was working, she overheard a couple at the next table talking about their upcoming wedding and she couldn't resist asking about their plans. They beamed with excitement as they shared their vision for a small, intimate ceremony with their closest family and friends. Every word the couple said reminded Dorothy of Moriah and Peter, and without even thinking about it, she smiled and offered to cater their wedding reception at the café, knowing Henry wouldn't have a problem with it. They eagerly accepted, and Dorothy added a note to her notepad to start planning the menu before reassuring them that it would be a special and memorable occasion.

As the café started to clear out, Dorothy found herself taking a moment to reflect on the day. She was grateful for the opportunity to serve others, to be a part of their lives even in a small way. This was what God meant her to do - to create a warm and welcoming space where people could come together and share a meal, a laugh, and even their deepest thoughts and feelings.

With a renewed sense of purpose, Dorothy headed back into the kitchen, ready to start planning the couple's special wedding event.

Knowing that she was doing God's will with her work in the café made a huge difference to Dorothy's peace of mind. The next morning, she woke up early, feeling excited for the day ahead. She put on her nicest dress, which was light blue, and carefully twisted her hair into a neat bun before pinning her *kapp* in place. She fastened her apron and then walked down the stairs into the café before unlocking the door with a smile on her face.

As soon as she flipped over the sign to say the café was open, people started coming in. She greeted each one with a warm hello and a smile. The regulars, like Mrs. Miller, greeted her back with a friendly wave and headed straight to their usual tables. New customers were always welcomed with a brief introduction to the menu and some recommendations.

Within minutes of opening the doors, the smell of freshly brewed coffee and baking pastries filled the air. Dorothy hummed a tune as she wiped down the counters and made sure everything was tidy. She enjoyed the sound of the customers chatting and laughing amongst themselves.

At one point, a group of children came in with their parents, and Dorothy couldn't help but grin. She loved seeing the little ones and the way their eyes lit up at the sight of the colorful cupcakes and muffins in the display case. Most of the time, she was able to have a quick chat with them. Dorothy would ask about their favorite sweets and joke with them. The parents would thank her, impressed with her kindness and hospitality.

As the days went on, and more and more people came in and out of the café. Dorothy continually found herself smiling.

She loved the rush of a busy day and the satisfaction of serving good food to happy customers. Even when she was tired, she kept going, fueled by the joy of her work.

At the end of the day, as the last customers would leave, Dorothy would take a deep breath and look around the café. It was quiet, but she could still feel the warmth and energy of the people who were there only moments before. She would turn off the lights and head up the stairs, feeling content and fulfilled.

Dorothy's heart raced as she read Saul's latest letter, feeling a deeper connection with him than she'd experienced before. She was still a bit anxious over how much she'd opened up to him, sharing parts of herself that she'd kept hidden away for so long, but as she read his warm letter, her nerves faded. She longed for more time with him, to see him in person and to feel his warmth and presence.

Despite her constantly busy schedule at the café, Dorothy couldn't help but daydream about spending time with Saul. She imagined walking through the park with him, talking about their dreams and hopes for the future. She imagined him sitting across from her at the café, sipping coffee and laughing at her jokes.

One day, as she was serving two customers, Dorothy looked up and saw Saul at the café's front door. Her heart skipped a beat, and she could hardly believe it was him. They greeted each other, like teenagers with a crush, and she felt an indescribable warmth spread through her.

"Hello, Dorothy," Saul said. "Sorry I haven't come here for a while, but things have been busy."

"You're here now and that's what matters," Dorothy replied as her heart swelled with gratitude and joy.

They talked for a while since there weren't many customers right then, and Saul asked about the café's daily operations, again showing a genuine interest in her work and how things were run.

"You know, I've been thinking," Saul said, as he looked at Dorothy intently. "With each day that passes in the fields, I find myself realizing that farming really isn't my calling."

Dorothy felt a thrill of excitement run through her as he spoke. She didn't know if he was serious, but the possibility of him becoming a café worker was too good to ignore.

"I would love it if we could work together," she said, smiling. "I'm sure we could make the café even better."

"We'll see," Saul said mysteriously, before changing the subject. They chatted about this and that, and Dorothy was grateful that talking to him was as easy as breathing.

As he left the café a short while later, Saul promised to write to her again soon, and Dorothy was left feeling both exhilarated and melancholic. She yearned for more time with him, but she knew the distance between them was a reality they must face. She returned to work, trying her best to focus on the customers and her duties, but her mind kept wandering back to Saul.

Chapter Eleven

Dorothy was serving customers at the café the next day when she saw Saul talking to Henry out of the corner of her eye. She couldn't hear what they were saying, but their body language suggested a serious conversation, and she couldn't help but wonder what it was about.

As she was clearing the table, Saul came up to her.

"Hello, again, Dorothy," Saul said. "I haven't gotten around to writing to you yet. How's your day been going?"

"Even better now that you're here," she replied, returning his smile. "What were you talking to Henry about?"

Saul's smile faltered for a moment before he composed himself. "Oh, just some ... stuff. Nothing for you to worry about."

Dorothy didn't press the issue, sensing Saul didn't want to talk about it.

"Do you want to go for ice cream?" Saul blurted out after a few moments of silence between them. "Henry says you have this evening off."

"That sounds wonderful *gut*," Dorothy agreed, delighted at the idea. She quickly finished up with her last customer before they walked to the ice cream shop down the street, chatting and laughing along the way.

Saul ordered a mint chocolate chip ice cream, while Dorothy chose a lemon sorbet.

As they were eating their sweet treats, Saul turned to her, a serious expression on his face. "Dorothy, I have to ask you something. Something I've asked multiple times before, and no matter what your answer is, I'm never giving up."

"All right," she replied as she licked the deliciously cool citrus flavor off her spoon.

"Can I court you?"

Dorothy hadn't expected this, although, she should have worked it out from how he'd phrased his words.

He went on. "Can we please think about a deeper relationship? I care about you a lot, *nee*, actually Dorothy, I love you. And I would like us to be together."

Dorothy's heart raced. Her feelings for Saul had developed over their correspondence, but she hadn't dared hope he'd ask to court her again after the numerous occasions she'd turned him down.

"*Jah,* Saul, I would like that very much," she told him, a smile spreading across her face.

Saul let out his breath in a whoosh. "*Ach,* I can't believe it. You said *jah.* I'm right glad, Dorothy. I've been wanting to ask you again for a while now."

Dorothy had never felt so happy and excited before. She wondered what had happened to the girl she used to be, the one who was afraid of taking risks and becoming involved.

Saul then took a deep breath as he poked his spoon into his melting dessert before telling her his plans. "I have some more news, and I hope you're going to like it," he said, looking at her with a mix of excitement and nerves.

Dorothy's heart quickened. "What is it?"

"I've decided to stay in town for a while," he replied, a small smile tugging at his lips.

Dorothy's eyes widened. "Truly? But that's wonderful *gut,*" she exclaimed. "But what about the farm and your family?"

Saul shrugged. "My brothers have always shown more of an interest in farming than I ever have. And I can visit my family often. Moriah has been missing you terribly."

"And I miss her," Dorothy replied as she inclined her head.

There was a moment of silence as Saul licked his spoon. "There's more. Henry and I have been talking, and he wants to step back from the café. He's not ready to sell it, but he wants to mentor me to take over as the manager."

Dorothy could hardly believe her ears. "You're going to be running the café? That's ... that's ... well, that's wonderful."

Saul grinned. "*We're* going to be running the café," he corrected her gently. "If it works out, Henry wants to take a long cross-country trip in his trailer, leaving the two of us in charge."

Dorothy's heart swelled with happiness. "I never thought I'd have a partner to run a café with, and now I have you."

Saul's smile widened. "I couldn't be more excited. Since watching you, I've loved the idea of running a café, and I couldn't think of anyone I'd rather do it with than you."

Saul's excitement was infectious, and Dorothy could hardly contain her joy. "This is going to be amazing," she said, unable to stop the excited bounce in her chair at the prospect of their future together.

Saul reached across the table and took her hand. Dorothy's breath caught with pleasure. Feeling his touch for the first time was everything she imagined and more. "I can't wait to see what we can do together."

A few hours later, Saul walked Dorothy back to the café. They'd lost track of time as they excitedly discussed their future together at the café and only started making their way back after the ice cream shop closed. Dorothy felt as though she were walking on air. She could hardly believe the man she had been writing to and yearning for wanted to work with her, too.

As they walked, they continued to talk about their hopes and dreams, sharing stories from their pasts. As always, it felt like they had known each other forever.

Once they reached the café's door, Saul took her hand and looked into her eyes. Dorothy tried to focus on his next words, but the feeling of his fingers around hers was almost too much to bear. "Dorothy, I can't wait to spend more time with you. You're a *gut* woman, and I feel so lucky to know you."

Dorothy felt her heart flutter at his words, and she couldn't help but smile. "I feel the same way, Saul. I can't believe this is happening," she replied, feeling giddy. "Who knew we would end up together after me turning you down so many times?"

"Life is funny that way," Saul replied as he gently squeezed her fingers in his own. "And I'm sure your *mamm* is looking down on us approvingly from heaven."

"Oh, of that I have no doubt," Dorothy replied with a laugh as she recalled her mother insisting she settle down and start a family. Back then, all Dorothy had felt about the idea was anxiety, but now, all she was feeling was peace, love, and excitement at the prospect of starting a life with Saul.

Saul leaned in to give her a gentle kiss on her cheek before saying goodnight. Dorothy watched him walk away, feeling grateful for this happy turn of events.

As she headed inside, she couldn't help thinking again of her mother. Bernice would have been thrilled for her, and Dorothy felt her presence at that moment more than she had since she lost her. She sat down at her desk, picked up a pen, and began to write a letter to Moriah, wanting to share the news of her newfound happiness.

With Saul by her side, Dorothy felt like anything was possible. She was excited to see where their courtship would take them, and she couldn't wait to spend more time getting to know him better.

Epilogue

One Year Later

The sun was shining down on the small town of Brewster as Dorothy walked hand-in-hand with her husband. A year had passed since she and Saul had first started courting. Within six months, they had been happily wed.

Now they strolled to the storefront of the café that meant so much to her, which now proudly displayed a notice that read, *Henry's Café: Under New Management.* She and Saul had taken over the business, just as Henry had hoped they would.

They stepped inside, and the aroma of freshly brewed coffee and sweet baked goods swirled around them. The place was bustling with customers, just like always, some of whom they'd come to know well over the past year.

Dorothy inhaled deeply and looked around with a smile. It was hard to believe that a year ago, she had been struggling to decide whether to leave her old life behind. But *ach*, how glad she was that she had followed her heart and left. Now, she had a loving husband, a wonderful café business, and a new sense of purpose. She breathed out with contentment as she rubbed the small, growing bump protruding from her belly.

She and Saul made their way to the back of the café where Henry sat at a table with a map spread out before of him. He looked up and grinned as they approach. "Hey, you two. Where's my coffee?"

"You're not my boss anymore," Dorothy quipped with a laugh as she went to the counter to pour him a cup. She handed his drink to him, and he leaned in and said, "You know, I'm thinking about taking that cross-country trip soon. You two will be able to handle things here, won't you?"

Saul chuckled and nodded. "Of course, Henry. We've got this, though I'm not sure why you're asking since we will soon own the place..."

Henry shrugged, looking sheepish. "Old habits die hard and all that. This place is still my old girl." He traced his finger over a scratch on the table. "I want to see her in good hands."

"You don't need to worry about a thing," Dorothy said, and she again gazed around the café, pride surging through her.

Running a café was hard work; it always had been, but she loved it.

She laid a hand gently on her belly. She would be eternally grateful for the opportunity she had to share all this with Saul. As the two of them sat down at the table with Henry, she knew they'd created something special. Something they would be happy with for many years to come.

"Tell me more about your trip," she asked Henry affectionately. "It's going to be wonderful. I just know."

The End

Continue Reading...

Thank you for reading **The Amish Cafe.** Are you wondering **what to read next?** Why not read **Helping Joel?** **Here's a peek for you:**

"Careful with that bucket, Marty," Joel warned his stepbrother, holding his breath as he watched his younger brother nearly topple over his head to feed one of the work horses.

"I am," Marty shot back, his voice coming out in a defensive snort. The six-year-old had been bound and determined to be more help after his father, Walter, had passed.

It was the second loss of a father for Joel, having lost his own father when he was a young boy. His mother had remarried Walter when Joel was twelve, and Joel had been blessed with

Walter stepping in and helping him through his vital years as a growing young man. But now, he, too, was gone.

And now I have to step in for my bruders.

Joel let out a sigh, removing his hat from his head to run his fingers through his dark brown hair. The weight of his new responsibilities hung heavy on his shoulders, and sometimes it felt as though the burden was much too heavy to carry. He loved his family, and it was downright painful watching his mother, Susannah, struggle so much with caring for everything on her own. Joel had inherited his birth-father's farm and had already been working overtime to try and make it profitable, but now that Walter had passed, he was the only family member capable of continuing to farm this land as well.

Two farms.

One man.

It was *not* a good combination, and Joel felt nothing but exhaustion as he toiled day in and day out. Joel's eyes wandered to his young brother, a trail of spilled feed following him as he finally made it to the stall to dump the grain in for the fatigued horses.

"Got it," Marty chirped, turning back to smile at Joel. "See, I'm real *gut* help if you just give me a chance. *Mamm* says that in a few years, I'll be just as strong as you."

Joel chuckled, shaking his head at the middle boy of the youngest three. "You'll get there one of these days," he said, giving his brother a smile.

Hopefully sooner rather than later.

"I bet it's time to eat some supper, don't you think?" Marty asked, his eyes falling to the setting sun. Joel nodded, his own gaze landing on the beautiful Ohio sunset, the warm glow illuminating the fields. However, he hardly had the time to admire its beauty—it was also a reminder he was running out of time to get everything done for the day.

VISIT HERE To Read More!

https://www.ticahousepublishing.com/amish-miller.html

Thank you for Reading

If you **love Amish Romance**, **Visit Here:**

https://amish.subscribemenow.com/

to find out about all **New Hannah Miller Amish Romance Releases! We will let you know as soon as they become available!**

If you enjoyed ***The Amish Cafe,*** would you kindly take a couple minutes to leave a positive review on Amazon? It only takes a moment, and positive reviews truly make a difference. I would be so grateful! Thank you!

Turn the page to discover more Hannah Miller Amish Romances just for you!

More Amish Romance from Hannah Miller

Visit HERE for Hannah Miller's Amish Romance

https://ticahousepublishing.com/amish-miller.html

About the Author

Hannah Miller has been writing Amish Romance for the past seven years. Long intrigued by the Amish way of life, Hannah has traveled the United States, visiting different Amish communities. She treasures her Amish friends and enjoys visiting with them. Hannah makes her home in Indiana, along with her husband, Robert. Together, they have three children and seven grandchildren. Hannah loves to ride bikes in the sunshine. And if it's warm enough for a picnic, you'll find her under the nearest tree!

Made in United States
Troutdale, OR
07/22/2024

21482310R00064